P9-DVM-969

the INCREDIBLE
Twisting
Arm
the Magic Shop

Kate Egan
with Magician Mike Lane
illustrated by Eric Wight

A FEIWEL AND FRIENDS BOOK
An Imprint of Macmillan

 Printed in the United States of America by R. R. Donnelley & Sons Company, Harrisonburg, Virginia. For information, address Feiwel and Friends, 175 Fifth Avenue, New York, N.Y. 10010.

Feiwel and Friends books may be purchased for business or promotional use. For information on bulk purchases, please contact the Macmillan Corporate and Premium Sales Department at (800) 221-7945 x5442 or by email at specialmarkets@macmillan.com

Library of Congress Cataloging-in-Publication Data Available

ISBN: 978-1-250-02915-7 [hardcover] / 978-1-250-04044-2 [paperback]
978-1-250-06027-3 [ebook]

Book design by Véronique Lefèvre Sweet

Feiwel and Friends logo designed by Filomena Tuosto

First Edition: 2014

1 3 5 7 9 10 8 6 4 2

mackids.com

For Jonathan, Maddie, and Nate,
who make magic every day.
—K. E.

To Donna, Lindsay, and Dan, real magic comes
from the heart. It's your support and encouragement
that make anything possible!
—M. L.

Chapter 1

THE REWARD

Friday afternoon. The end of another long week of fourth grade.

The principal hadn't called Mike's parents. Not even once. Mike had earned two green tickets for being a good citizen of his classroom, and no red tickets for poor choices. He'd finished his homework on time and sat through the Friday spelling test. But man, was he tired. And it felt like he was getting a cold. Mike

Mike
SPELLING

didn't know how Nora, his next-door neighbor, handled being a model student week after week. Maybe it was easier if you were a genius.

The car slowed down and Mike's mom pulled into a parking spot just as a bleep announced she had a new text. "Why don't you go on without me?" she said to Mike. "I'll be there in a second."

Good thing, because he couldn't wait much longer. He'd been counting the hours since Monday. His reward for a smooth week? A trip to The White Rabbit, the local magic shop. To Mike, it was better than a ride on a roller coaster. Better than a week of snow days. Better than an ice-cream sundae! He practically ran to the door.

Anyone walking into The White Rabbit for the first time might think it was an antiques shop or a flea market. That's what Mike had thought, anyway. It was full of dusty furniture and things you might find in someone's attic after they died. All that stuff was sort of awesomely mysterious. But the best part about The White Rabbit was a little room, hidden in the back. It was full of equipment for magic tricks!

It turned out that the owner of The White Rabbit, Mr. Zerlin, was a magician. Did that mean he was a guy who could do tricks? Or a guy who had magic powers? Mike still didn't know. But there was one thing he knew for sure. For some reason, Mr. Zerlin was convinced that he—Mike!—could be a magician too. It was like some sixth sense allowed Mr. Zerlin to see something special about him. No wonder Mike was grinning as the door shut behind him.

"Hey, Mike!" said a teenager behind the counter. Carlos was here most afternoons. You'd call it a part-time job, except it wasn't like any job Mike had ever heard of. Mostly what Carlos did was play with the magic stuff, show it off for customers, and practice new tricks.

Mike's smile grew even bigger. Carlos knew his name now!

"Want to see something cool?" Carlos asked. "I just can't figure this out."

He came out from behind the counter and walked to a nearby table. Carlos wiped the dust off with the arm of his sweatshirt. Then he put his right hand down horizontally on the table, fingers facing toward the left. Slowly, he began to twist the hand toward his body.

"Okay . . ." said Mike. He didn't get it. Carlos wasn't doing anything unusual at all.

"I bet you can do that," Carlos admitted. "But can you do *this*? I'm pretty sure this isn't normal. Maybe I'm double-jointed or something—I don't know."

Mike knew a kid who was double-jointed. He didn't know what that meant, exactly, except that the kid could bend his thumb all the way back until it touched his wrist. He did it on purpose, to freak people out.

So he watched as Carlos kept twisting his hand, a little more slowly. It was facing toward the right now. It looked like it hurt, but Carlos kept twisting. And twisting. And twisting . . . until the hand went all the way around, like a hand on a clock. There was a terrible cracking sound while he did it. That double-jointed kid couldn't do anything like this! No one could—outside of a horror movie.

Carlos stood up and shook his hand in the air. "Ugh," he said. "Hurts like crazy. Can you believe that?"

A part of Mike knew that Carlos had fooled him. It was impossible, what he did! But Mike loved that moment when he wasn't sure, when he didn't know how a magic trick worked.

"Great effect!" said Mike. That was how magicians gave each other a compliment.

Then he sort of stood there, waiting. Hoping.

Outside The White Rabbit, Carlos would never tell how the effect worked. That was an important part of being a magician: keeping the secrets secret. Inside the store, though, magicians shared their tips and tricks all the time. Mr. Zerlin had taught Mike some illusions step by step. Maybe Carlos would teach him, too?

But no. The phone rang and Carlos ran for it and Mike tried not to be disappointed.

His mom came in with a paper cup from the coffee shop across the street. "Did you find anything you want to buy?" she asked.

"Not yet," said Mike. "I haven't even started looking!" That was when he headed for the room in the back. His mom wouldn't get him anything too expensive, he knew, but she'd be good for a new deck of cards. Or maybe a wand.

It was just so hard to choose! If Mr. Zerlin were here, he might be able to help. But Mike didn't see him anywhere.

While Mike poked around, his mom stayed in the front of the shop, peering into a case of old jewelry. Carlos was moving furniture, trying to make some space in the middle of the floor. After a while, he set up some folding chairs. Mike could hear them clanking together.

"So, are you guys coming tomorrow?" Carlos asked Mrs. Weiss.

"What's happening tomorrow?" Mike's mom said.

"At three o'clock, we're having a special show by a visiting magician," Carlos replied. "An expert in transformations."

That was turning one thing into another, Mike remembered. Like a blue silk handkerchief into a red one. Or an eight of clubs into a six of hearts. He didn't know how to do that yet. He *wished* he knew how to do that. But the Weisses were busy tomorrow.

"We have other plans," he heard his mom say. "Sorry, but we just can't make it. Maybe another time." Mike didn't even get a chance to speak for himself.

It was his grandma's birthday. She was coming for dinner with his aunt and uncle and cousins. A pair of tiny twins. Okay, it wasn't as bad as it sounded. Mike didn't have brothers or sisters, so his cousins were the next best thing. Plus he was crazy about his grandma. But he wanted to see the magician, and he knew there was no chance it would ever happen now. His parents always made a big deal out of birthdays.

He picked out a trick he hadn't learned yet—a set of blue cups and red foam balls—and walked glumly toward the counter to pay. Carlos was still chatting with his mom.

"Supposed to get cold tonight," Carlos said, almost like he was a grown-up.

Carlos was just a kid, though. He came to The White Rabbit on his bike after school. He wasn't even old enough to drive.

Suddenly, Mike thought of something. If Carlos could do that, maybe he could do it, too. Ride his bike into town, all by himself. He'd had one good week, right? If he had a few more good weeks, maybe his mom and dad would trust him to come to The White Rabbit on his own.

If he was ever going to be a magician, he couldn't wait around for his parents, right? The more Mike thought about it, the more he was convinced. If he had his way, he'd never miss another magic show again. He'd be a regular at the shop. In no time, Carlos would be sharing secrets with him, too!

Mike turned around and walked back into the magic room. He'd get those cups and balls another time. Today, there was something else he needed.

On one shelf there was a little section of stuff that was supposed to bring you good luck. Mike bent down to take a close look at what was there. Four-leaf clovers. Horseshoes. There were even some rabbit's foot keychains. . . . Not so lucky for the rabbits, Mike thought. But whatever.

The horseshoe was small enough to stick in the pocket of his backpack, but big enough so it wouldn't get lost. Mike knew, because he lost stuff all the time.

"Ready?" his mom said as soon as she spotted him. She was at the counter with her wallet.

"Ready," said Mike. Ready to leave, since he had to. But mostly ready to work on his plan: becoming the new Mike. Like the Mike he'd been all week . . . only better. Mature, responsible, totally trustworthy.

He'd need all the good luck he could get.

Chapter 2
HELP ME!

Mike's parents always liked to get advice from experts. If they had a problem with their sink, they wouldn't just call a plumber. They'd find a Master Plumber. When Mike needed extra help in math, they made sure he got Mr. Malone, who also taught kids at the high school. Mike's parents trusted people who were the best of the best.

And Mike happened to know the local expert on being mature and responsible!

She had straight Es on her last report card for "exceeds expectations." Her parent-teacher conference was practically a party. She was Mike's new friend, Nora, who lived right next door. He saw her every day. Maybe she'd know what he had to do to impress his parents and earn a new privilege.

Mike's mom and dad were in the kitchen. Their guests would be arriving in a couple of hours, and his parents had just come home with the groceries. Now they were rushing around, getting things ready. It was a good time to stay out of their way.

"I'll be in the yard!" Mike said on his way out. He crossed the stretch of grass between his house and Nora's, and rang her doorbell. When she came to the door, Mike said, "Hey, want to come over for a while?"

Nora disappeared inside to ask if it was okay, then ran back, her ponytail flying out

REPORT CARD
1 2 3 4
READING
SCIENCE
ART
MUSIC
LIBRARY
COMPUTER
Miss Manners
ATTENDANCE
1 2 3 4
Absent
0 0 0 0
Tardy
0 0 0 0

behind her. "Should I bring anything with me?" she asked. Sometimes she and Mike worked on magic tricks together after school.

"No magic right now," Mike said. "Actually, I need a little advice."

Nora zipped up her jacket and gave him a funny look as they crossed back into his yard. "About what?" she asked.

"It's just that there's a magic show at The White Rabbit today, and I have to miss it. It's my grandma's birthday, and my relatives are all coming for dinner."

Mike sat down on one of his swings, and Nora sat on the one next to him. "So you want me to . . . find a way to get you to the store?"

"Not exactly," Mike said. Not even Nora could do that. "But I'm making a plan to get there next time. If I can show my parents I'm mature and responsible, maybe they'll let me ride my bike downtown by myself."

Nora thought about it for a minute. "My parents would never go for that," she said, shaking her head.

Nora's parents were stricter than Mike's. They were into organic food and limited screen time. "I know," said Mike. "But I think my parents would like it if I could do things on my own. It's just that they don't think they can trust me."

"So you need to change their minds," Nora said.

It was good that she always understood things so quickly. "Yeah," said Mike. "So what do you think I should do?"

It was a little embarrassing to be asking, actually. What if someone walked by and overheard them? Mike's house was on the corner, so his yard wasn't in the back of the house. More like right on the street.

Nora thought it over. "You could help out around the house a little," she said. "Do some extra chores." Nora knew all about chores, so Mike listened carefully. "Empty the dishwasher. Put away your laundry. That sort of thing."

"Yeah," Mike said again. It didn't sound that exciting.

"Yard work?" suggested Nora. "Keep your room clean?"

This plan was sounding way too hard. And that was before Nora made her worst suggestion of all. "Bring home a really good report card?"

Mike just stared at her. "I bet you could do it," Nora said optimistically.

How could she even think that? Mike wondered. They were together every day after school. She'd seen him struggle with multiplication and book reports. He never exceeded expectations. His report card always said "needs improvement."

"I'm just saying," Nora said. "That would change your parents' minds for sure."

"Okay," said Mike. "I'll think about it."

It was time to change the subject.

"So . . . there's this new trick I want to try," he said, taking a deck of cards out of his pocket. "It's a cool one. But I'm going to need a partner."

Her eyes lit up. "I could be your partner."

"Great!" said Mike. That was exactly what he hoped she'd say. Nora was the only person he'd trust with a secret like this. With magic, though, *he* was the expert. "I'll tell you how it works!"

Mike had learned the trick from *The Book of Secrets,* the amazing book that Mr. Zerlin had given him soon after they met. First a spectator would pick a card and Mike would look at it. Then he'd make a big announcement: He knew someone with magical powers so great that they could tell what the card was . . . over the phone!

"So you'll be the mysterious friend," Mike explained. "Your name is Ms. Magus—that means sorcerer. I'll call you on the phone and ask you to identify the card. Really, though, I'll be *telling* you what the card is, using a code we work out ahead of time. Once you know what it is, you'll talk to the spectator on the phone, and tell them what the card is. Then, you know, the person will faint from the shock."

He was kidding about that last part. But Nora wasn't laughing. Suddenly Mike noticed she was waving to someone in the street.

It was Emily Winston and her mom—they lived down the block—walking their beagle, Pookie. They weren't Mike's favorite neighbors, but he followed Nora over to say hello.

Pookie sniffed Mike's hand. "Gentle," Mrs. Winston cautioned, like she always did. Long ago, he'd pulled the dog's tail, and Mrs. Winston had never forgotten. Mike would always be five years old to her. Not old enough to bike downtown. Not even off training wheels! Pretty soon, though, she'd see how Mike had changed.

Emily barely even looked at Mike. She was all about Nora. "What are you doing later?" Emily asked, girl to girl. "Want to come over after we finish walking the dog?"

Mike glared at Emily. Nora was at *his* house right now. They were in the middle of something important!

But Nora turned to Mike and said, "You're having guests, right?" And what could he say? It was true.

"Sure!" said Nora. "I'll tell my dad. Want me to bring my jump rope?"

Emily nodded, like she and Nora jump-roped together all the time. As she walked away with Pookie, Mike wished he could make her disappear.

Nora was really making friends with Emily Winston? Mike couldn't believe it. Emily was the kind of kid who always shushed him when he forgot to raise his hand at school. Could one person be friends with both him and her? Mike was pretty sure that was impossible.

He tried to shake it off. Get back to the trick. He still needed to tell Nora the code. And there was another problem, too.

"How am I going to make the call to Ms. Magus?" he asked, like they had never stopped talking. Some kids his age had cell phones, but not Mike. Not Nora, either. Maybe she'd have some good ideas?

Before she could answer, he heard his mom. "Mike!" she called. "Could you set the table for me, please?"

He really didn't want to. But one look at Nora reminded him: The new Mike was mature and responsible. Just like her.

"Sure!" he called back, super-helpful.

And even though he hated to do it, he used the same cheerful voice to say good-bye to Nora. "Gotta go," he said. "Have fun at Emily's!"

Chapter 3
FAMILY PARTY

Mike took extra care with the table. He folded the napkins. He made sure there were enough chairs. He wasn't sure where he was supposed to put the forks and knives, but he did the best he could.

From the dining-room window, Mike could see his aunt's car pull into his driveway. His grandma stepped out of the front seat, carrying a bag of presents. But she was

the one with the birthday, Mike thought. So who were they for? He went outside to check things out.

Mike gave a cautious wave to Aunt Susan and Uncle Jim. They sometimes asked that question that adults loved to ask: "How's school?" He had an agreement with his grandma, though, that she would never ask unless he brought it up first.

Her face lit up when she saw him. "Mike!" she said, wrapping him into a gentle bear hug. "You've grown about a foot!" Grown-ups always said that, too, but it was okay. Her bright red sweater was soft against Mike's face.

Two small bodies burst out of the backseat. "Boo!" shouted Jake and Lily at the same time. "We scared you, Mike? Right?"

The twins were wearing costumes, even though Halloween was last week. Jake was a firefighter and Lily was a princess.

Mike remembered when he was five, like them. He could never get enough of his costume, either. And he still loved jumping out at people to scare them, even though other fourth graders thought it was annoying.

Before he could even talk to his grandma, the twins were begging him to play. Jake spotted a pile of leaves Mike's dad had raked. He leaped into the middle and called, "Come on, Mike!"

Nora hadn't mentioned it, but Mike knew that some kids their age helped take care of their younger brothers and sisters. If he helped out with the twins, it could send the right message to his parents. They'd see him taking charge . . . practically a grown-up himself! After that, how could they keep him from riding his bike to The White Rabbit?

Monster Chase was one of his favorite games when he was little. Mike was sure his cousins would love it too. Once the adults went inside, he turned to them. "I'm gonna get you!" he growled. "Grrr!"

His fingers were claws and his roar was as loud as a freight train! Mike chased Jake and Lily onto the porch and up to the top of the swing set. They hid in the bushes until he launched a sneak attack. "You can't catch us!" they yelled.

He chased them around the grill and to the fence at the edge of the grass.

Then Mike's mom opened the back door. "Mike," she said. He could tell from her voice that he'd done something wrong. "Don't get them all worked up, okay?" she said so Jake and Lily couldn't hear. "We'll never calm them down before dinner."

Man, thought Mike. "I was just trying to help," he said.

"Let's try something a little quieter," Mrs. Weiss said. "Maybe a board game?" She closed the door and went back inside.

Well, that sounded seriously boring.

Lily was at Mike's elbow. "Again!" she said. "Let's do it again!"

He had to think fast. He grabbed the rake and added a new layer of crispy leaves to the leaf pile. "Hang on a sec," he told the twins. "Watch this!"

Mike climbed onto one of his swings and got it going as high as he could. Then he jumped off, flew across the yard—and crash-landed in the leaves!

"My turn!" Jake and Lily both shouted. Jake went first and landed right in the middle of the pile, with leaves stuck in his hair. Lily kind of skidded over the edge of it, so Mike had to rake the leaves up again. He'd make the pile taller and higher, he decided. Bigger and better!

Suddenly, his mom was back on the porch. "That's too dangerous, Mike!" she said sharply. "Someone could get hurt!"

Mike sighed. This wasn't going well. Instead of proving he was mature or responsible, he was proving that he was full of bad ideas.

Stalling for time, Mike pushed Jake on the swing. "Hey—I really like your costume," he told his cousin.

"I'm going to be a firefighter when I grow up," Jake said. He paused and looked at Mike. "What are you going to be when you grow up?"

Mike had already figured that out, of course. "A magician," he said.

Jake's eyes opened wide. "Do you know any magic?" he said.

Mike grinned. *Now* he knew what to do with the twins. If he couldn't go to the show, he'd *do* a show! "Sure I do," he said. "You want to see?" His cousins nodded quickly, like a pair of bobblehead dolls.

"Okay . . . why don't you guys wait inside while I get my things ready," he said. While Mike headed to his room, Jake and Lily settled down on the bench in the Weisses' front hallway.

He was learning magic tricks steadily, but not all of them were ready to show off. He had to practice pretty hard to get them right, to make sure that no one could tell how they were done. But he had a couple of cool illusions ready to go at a moment's notice. He came back downstairs with a deck of cards and a large cardboard box.

Mike put the box on the floor and shuffled the cards. It was a little strange to go from being a monster to being a magician. He took a deep breath, showed the cards to the twins, and put them in a stack on top of the box. "Ready to get started? Okay. You guys can pick three cards out of this deck."

Jake and Lily stepped forward and took the top three cards.

"Now give one to me," Mike said. "And you should each keep one for yourself, too. Got it?"

The twins nodded.

Mike held his index finger straight up, with the rest of his fingers curled down. "Can you both do this?" he asked.

When they were in position, Mike said, "Next, just do what I do." Mike took his card and balanced it on the tip of his finger. With his other hand, he steadied it until it was perfectly horizontal. "You want to keep it as straight as you can."

Jake needed a little help from his sister, but eventually they both managed to copy Mike.

"Now watch this," said Mike. He didn't say a magic word, because he didn't have a good one yet, but he paused for effect. Then he took his extra hand away, leaving the card to balance—alone—on his fingertip!

Lily's mouth opened. "Can I try?" she said. Mike nodded, and she took away the extra hand, but her card fluttered to the ground. The same thing happened to Jake.

"But . . . how did you do that?" Lily sputtered.

Mike shrugged. "Like I said," he replied. "Magic!"

Now he had their attention. And hopefully the grown-ups were paying attention too. He wasn't always loud or wild. He could be mature, when he needed to be. He could entertain a pair of little kids. He could be trusted.

"We're eating in a minute," his mom said, popping into the hallway.

Mike winked at his cousins. "You guys want to see something amazing before dinner?" he said. Mike lowered his voice, like he was telling them a secret. "I have a finger in a box."

He opened the big cardboard box and took out a smaller one, about the size of a pair of gloves. This was one of his favorite tricks. It creeped out his friends Zack and Charlie, every time.

With both hands, he waved the smaller box in front of the twins. "Which one of you dares to open it?" he said, like it was dangerous.

Jake jumped up. "I do!" he said. He opened the lid of the smaller box, and there it was! Sitting on a bed of cotton, looking old and wrinkly, was a lone human finger, covered in a fine white dust. Jake gazed at it, his mouth hanging open.

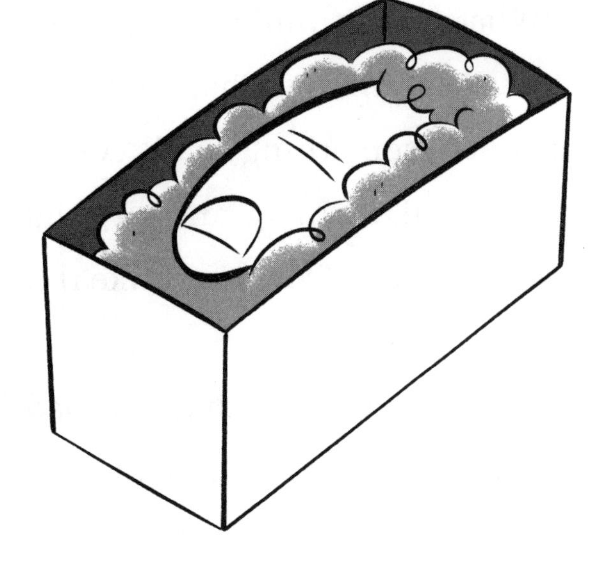

Mike dropped his voice a little lower. "And you know the most amazing thing about it? This finger is still alive!"

Gingerly, Jake touched it with his own finger. When he poked it, the finger moved!

Just then, Mike's mom came back. "Eeew!" she said, taking a couple of giant steps away from it. "What is that?"

"A severed finger," Mike said brightly, using the fanciest word he knew for "cut off."

"For a pair of kindergartners, Mike?" his mom said, frowning. She clapped the cover back on the box. "What are you thinking? That's enough!"

What was he thinking? That she was making a big deal out of something small. A mountain out of a molehill, as his grandma might say. When his mom wasn't looking, Mike rolled his eyes.

Then Lily understood what she had been looking at, and her eyes filled with tears. "It's someone's finger?" she said. "From a real hand? But that's scary!"

Mrs. Weiss looked at Mike. "What was wrong with a nice game of Candyland?" she asked.

As usual, Mike had ruined everything.

CREEPY FINGER

BEFORE YOU START THIS TRICK, YOU'LL NEED TWO CARDBOARD BOXES—ONE SMALL AND ONE LARGER—WITH TOPS.

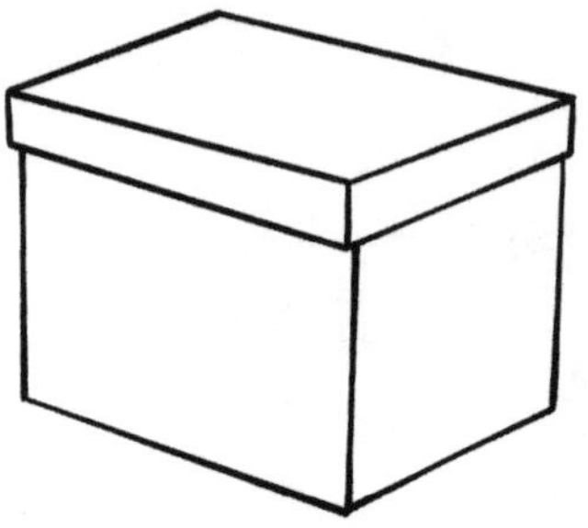

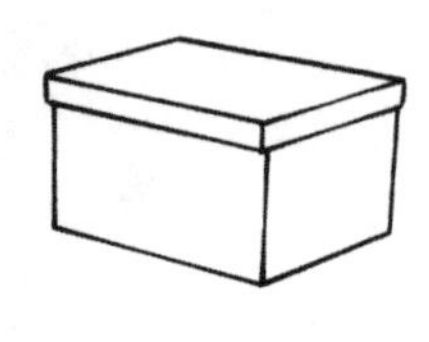

LINE THE INSIDE OF THE SMALLER BOX WITH COTTON WOOL, THEN PUT THE TOP ON IT.

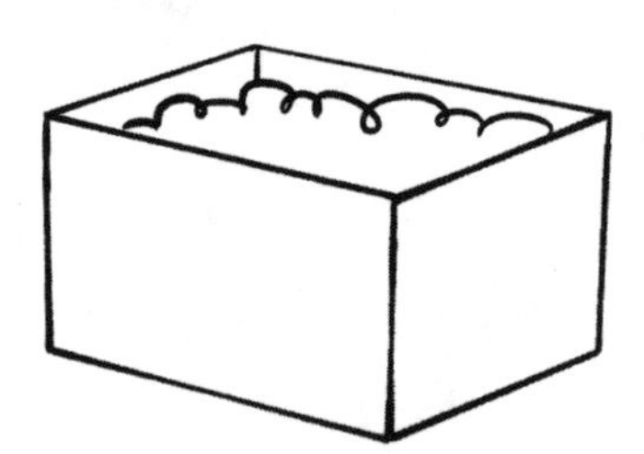

2.

NOW, TURN THAT BOX OVER AND CUT A SMALL HOLE IN THE BOTTOM. IT SHOULD BE JUST BIG ENOUGH TO SLIP A FINGER INTO DURING THE TRICK. THE COTTON WOOL WILL COVER THE HOLE.

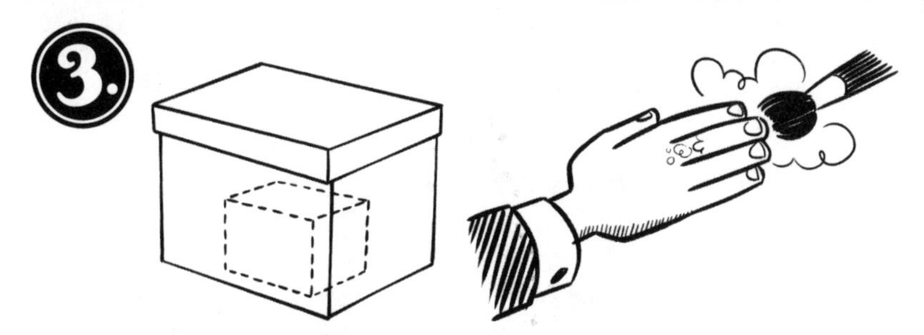

PUT THE SMALL BOX INTO THE LARGER BOX AND CLOSE IT. YOU'RE ALMOST READY! THE LAST THING TO DO BEFORE YOU START IS TO DUST THE BACK OF YOUR MIDDLE FINGER WITH BABY POWDER.

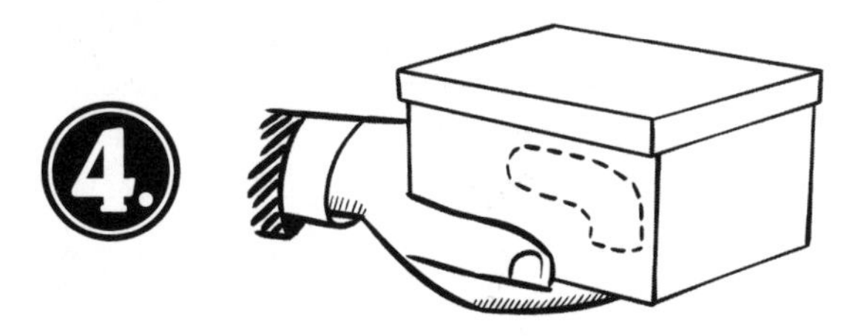

NOW, YOU CAN TELL YOUR AUDIENCE THAT YOU HAVE A FINGER IN A BOX. ASK THEM IF THEY WANT TO SEE IT! THEN OPEN THE LARGER BOX AND REMOVE THE SMALLER BOX WITH BOTH HANDS. MEANWHILE, SLIP YOUR POWDERED MIDDLE FINGER INTO THE HOLE YOU CUT INTO IT.

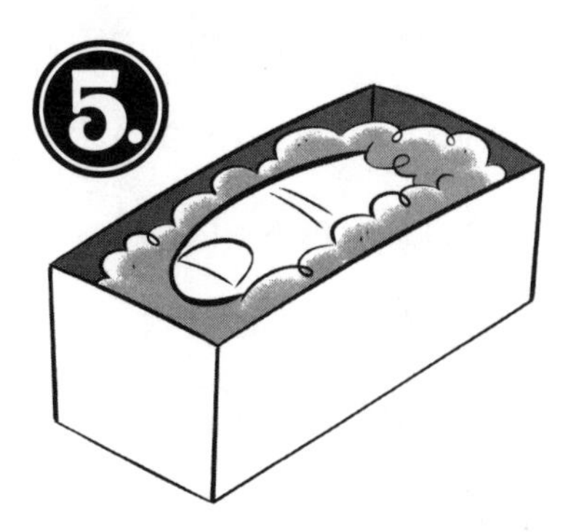

WITH YOUR OTHER HAND, SLOWLY REMOVE THE TOP FROM THE SMALLER BOX. INSIDE, YOUR AUDIENCE WILL SEE A LONE FINGER, GHOSTLY WHITE, LYING ON THE COTTON WOOL. CREEPY!

(YOU COULD ALSO INVITE A MEMBER OF THE AUDIENCE TO TOUCH THE FINGER. AND WHEN SHE DOES, THE FINGER WILL MOVE . . . JUST LIKE IT'S ALIVE!)

Chapter 4

TRY AGAIN

Mike sulked through dinner. Normally he would have loved a spaghetti feast. But what did it matter now? he thought. He would never be able to bike alone to the magic shop. For the rest of his life, he'd only be able to learn new magic when his parents were in the mood to take him there. And with their busy schedules? That wasn't going to happen very often.

Yeah, he could learn new techniques online. He could learn from *The Book of Secrets*. But that wasn't the same as getting to know real live magicians. He would never be part of their secret club.

Why did he have to mess everything up? It was like his teachers always said: He didn't know when to stop.

Lily wouldn't look at him, and Mike wouldn't look at his mom. But it was his grandma's birthday, so there was singing. And chocolate cake. And presents.

Grandma loved the gift he gave her: a book of card tricks. Then she said, "I have some presents for you kids, too. I hope nobody spoiled my surprise!"

Jake got a scooter, and Lily got a set of fairy wings. Mike waited until it was his turn, though he could hardly sit still. Finally, Grandma handed him a tall, thin box.

"There's a story behind this one," she said. "When I moved out of my old house last year, I almost left this behind. It had been in the basement for longer than I could remember."

Great, thought Mike. A recycled present.

"But it belonged to my cousin—he used it when he was young. And now that you're into magic . . . I'm glad I've kept it all this time!"

Mike ripped off the paper and opened the box. There was a tall, black hat, like something Abraham Lincoln would wear. It would make quite the fashion statement at school.

He put it on the coffee table and tried to look enthusiastic. It didn't quite stand up straight. If he ever wore this thing—which he wouldn't—it would be all lopsided, drooping to one side. What was his grandma thinking?

"Look inside!" she said.

When Mike peered into the bottom, he could see a small compartment sewn inside, next to the lining. He sighed with relief. He wasn't supposed to wear it. This was a magic hat! He'd been wanting one of these for a while.

He met his grandma's eyes, and she winked. She knew she shouldn't give it away.

Grandma smiled. "See anything there?"

Now Mike was confused. Was there something else, besides the compartment? He looked in one more time and he couldn't believe he'd missed it. An envelope . . . with plastic inside. A gift card to The White Rabbit!

Somehow, his grandma knew that what he really wanted wasn't just a *present.* It was the chance to go to a *place.* And now his parents

the White Rabbit
GIFT CERTIFICATE

would have to take him there. At least one more time.

"I promise not to get anything disturbing," Mike told his dad as they got out of the car the next day, in front of The White Rabbit. They'd had a long talk after his cousins left.

"Use your best judgment and you'll be fine," his dad said patiently. "I'll meet you in a little while." He was stopping in at a bookstore first , so Mike would have time to browse. They both knew he'd be safe at the magic shop.

Mike wiped his feet on the store's doormat. It said "Believe" in bright red letters.

As soon as he stepped inside, Mike could see the folding chairs still set up from yesterday's show. There was a poster still propped on a stand. "Welcome, Professor Mysterioso," it said.

"Master of Mystery!" There was a picture of the professor, with piercing eyes and a purple cape.

"We missed you yesterday," said a voice from the back of the store. Mr. Zerlin walked over to say hello.

He was wearing jeans and a dark red shirt. Today there were tiny cards embroidered on the front pocket—all aces. His look was half mad scientist, half crazy uncle. But something about him seemed more magical than Professor Mysterioso.

"My parents wouldn't drive me," Mike replied. "I had to be at a family party."

Mr. Zerlin nodded. He wasn't a big talker.

"But I have a plan to get here next time," Mike said. "Or I *had* a plan. . . ." Suddenly, he was babbling. "I thought that I could convince my parents I was mature and responsible. And then I could ride my bike here, by myself. Like Carlos. Only I'm not mature or responsible, and everyone knows it. So the plan was a disaster. And now I don't know what to do. But I don't want to miss another show!"

He could feel his face turning as red as Mr. Zerlin's shirt. For some reason, Mr. Zerlin thought that Mike exceeded expectations. But now he was seeing the real Mike. The one that needed improvement.

Then Mr. Zerlin walked over to the counter. Usually it was covered in stuff like order forms and bills. Today, though, there were some other things there. A big coffee cup, a bottle of water, and a bowl. Mr. Zerlin picked up the bottle of water and poured some into the cup.

"Instant ice!" he commanded it.

He dumped the water from the cup into the bowl. And suddenly it wasn't water anymore. It was a pile of ice cubes!

Mike was glad they didn't have to talk anymore. Mr. Zerlin knew he really just wanted to learn some magic. And unlike Carlos, Mr. Zerlin would share his secrets.

"Can you show me how you did that?" Mike asked.

Actually, it was very simple. There were already ice cubes in the coffee cup, but only the magician could see them. There was a small sponge underneath them too.

When Mr. Zerlin poured water into the mug, he was actually pouring it *over* the ice and *into* the sponge. The sponge soaked up the water, and the ice went into the bowl.

"Want to try?" asked Mr. Zerlin.

Mike grinned. Of course he did!

But when Mike tried, he poured in too much water. The sponge didn't absorb it all. Then, when he went to pour the ice from the bowl, the extra water sploshed all over the place. And some ice cubes tumbled to the floor. Another failure.

"Sorry," Mike mumbled.

"Try again," said Mr. Zerlin. "Only different."

Mr. Zerlin had a funny way of talking, like everything he said had two meanings at the same time. Was he talking about the trick? Mike wondered. Try it again, but a different way? He was looking at Mike so intently that Mike wondered if he was really talking about something else. Understanding Mr. Zerlin was like understanding Yoda in *Star Wars*. Mike had to think hard to get to the heart of what he said.

Could he be talking about Mike's plan to bike downtown?

Actually, Mike kind of liked the sound of "Try again, only different." There was some old expression that went, "If at first, you don't succeed . . . try, try again." Maybe working super-hard worked for people like Nora, but it wasn't enough for Mike. He just made the same mistakes all over again.

QUICK FREEZE

Before you're ready to perform this trick, put a slightly damp sponge in the bottom of a cup, making sure it fits tightly. Put a number of ice cubes on top of the sponge. Next, set a bottle of water and an empty clear bowl in front you on a table. Now, you're ready to start.

1. For this trick, it's important that you're standing up and your audience is sitting down. Since you're slightly above them, they won't be able to see inside of the cup.

HOLDING THE CUP IN FRONT OF YOU, POUR A LITTLE WATER INTO IT FROM THE BOTTLE. THE SPONGE IN THE BOTTOM WILL ABSORB THE WATER.
2.
3.
NOW, TIP THE CUP OVER THE EMPTY BOWL (KEEP THE CUP TIPPED TOWARD YOURSELF, ENSURING THE AUDIENCE CAN'T SEE INSIDE OF IT). THE ICE CUBES WILL TUMBLE OUT.
IN JUST A FEW SECONDS, YOU'VE TURNED WATER INTO ICE.

Trying a different way . . . that was something else. Maybe there was some *other* way to work on his parents? To earn the privilege of biking alone into town?

Mr. Zerlin put his hands up and shrugged, as if to say, "How could it hurt? It's worth a try." Like he was reading Mike's mind or something. It didn't make sense. But a part of Mike really believed that Mr. Zerlin was magical.

Then the door swung open and Mike's dad entered. It felt like Mike had only been here a few minutes, but apparently his dad had already browsed through the entire bookstore. It was almost time to go.

Mike picked out a stuffed bunny from the magic room—it was the perfect thing to go with his new hat. When he got to the counter, he could see that Mr. Zerlin had replaced the ice cubes and refilled the water.

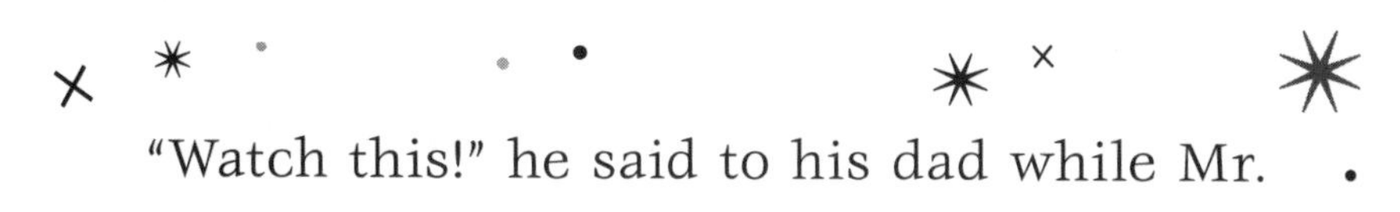

"Watch this!" he said to his dad while Mr. Zerlin rang up his order. This time, to Mike's relief, he got it right.

His dad's eyes widened. "Nice!" he said. "Better than an ice machine!" he joked.

Mr. Zerlin smiled at Mike's dad. "You have a very talented boy here," he said.

Mike's dad beamed. People didn't say that to him very often. "Why thank you," he said. "I don't even think we've officially met, though I've heard a lot about you." He held out his hand and said his name. "David Weiss."

Mr. Zerlin held his hand for a second, and gazed at him. "Like Houdini."

"Mike *is* getting to be a regular Houdini!" said Mr. Weiss.

"That's not what I meant," said Mr. Zerlin. "I meant that Weiss was the original name of Harry Houdini. The most famous magician the world has ever known." It was like he couldn't believe Mike's dad didn't know. "Houdini was named Erik Weisz when his family came to

America from Hungary. First he changed the spelling, then his whole name."

"I have the same last name as Houdini?" Mike said. Could they be related? "Did he have any kids?" he asked Mr. Zerlin hopefully.

"Houdini left no descendants," Mr. Zerlin said. "Only his wife. Still, Weiss is a perfect name for a young magician."

Mr. Weiss poked Mike with his elbow. "See? I'm always saying our family is something special."

It was the first good news Mike had had since he left school on Friday afternoon. The first time he felt even a little lucky. Hey, Mike thought, I still have that horseshoe in my backpack someplace. Maybe it's starting to work its magic for me? Better late than never.

Mike took a deep breath as he left the store. It was time for plan B. It was time to try again.

Chapter 5
PLAN B

Not that he actually had a plan B yet . . .

The school day had barely started, but Mike was ready for recess. Through the window beside his desk, he could see the clear blue sky of a perfect fall day. Two more hours until he'd be out there playing with Zack and Charlie. Two. Long. Hours.

His teacher, Mrs. Canfield, was wrapping up the morning meeting, making announcements, and delivering mail. Mike rolled some pencils back and forth across his desk until he felt a pair of eyes fixed on him. He looked up to meet the stare of Emily Winston. Nora's new friend. She was in Mike's class and sitting across from him.

"Sorry," Mike whispered. He didn't mean to bother her. He just liked the sound of the pencils: *clickety-click*. Like a train.

Mrs. Canfield clapped her hands in rhythm. *Clap, clap, clap-clap-clap.* Sometimes that was a signal that her class should be quiet, but right now it was the signal that they were moving on to something new.

The teacher smiled. "This morning, we're going to begin our new unit on everyday science," she said. "Using simple materials we find around the house—or in the classroom—we'll answer some scientific questions and study some scientific principles."

Mike sat up a little straighter.

"We'll start by making a volcano," said Mrs. Canfield. "With baking soda and vinegar, we can create an eruption right here in our classroom!" She had already constructed what looked like a mountain, by molding some dough around a plastic bottle.

She had Mike's full attention now. A volcano? In school? Awesome! He jumped out of his seat to get a better view. Then he saw Emily watching him again. Probably waiting for him to get in trouble.

Mrs. Canfield explained that the bottle was full of warm water. Now she poured in a little dish soap. "Let's also add some food coloring, so our lava looks true to life," she said, putting in several drops of red dye.

"Now for the most important ingredients," she said. Mrs. Canfield measured out some baking soda and vinegar.

Emily Winston raised her hand. She was taking lots of notes. "How much do you put in?" she asked.

"The measurements don't need to be exact," said Mrs. Canfield. "Just keep the amounts about even.

"Now, watch this closely. . . ." She poured the vinegar on top of the baking soda, and all of a sudden red suds oozed out of the volcano! The eruption didn't last for long, but it looked exactly like the real thing. Mike couldn't believe it was all over so fast.

Mrs. Canfield explained what had happened. "The vinegar and the baking soda reacted to create something new—a gas called carbon dioxide. And that gas pushed the suds out of the bottle."

She wrote it all out on the whiteboard. "What did it look like?" she asked the class.

"Like foam!" said Ben.

"Like slime!" said Jada.

Mrs. Canfield collected all the words in a list.

"All week we're going to do experiments like this at school," Mrs. Canfield continued. "You don't have to be in a lab to do science! Most of your homework will be writing short reports about what we've done in class. How did it happen? What did you see?"

Could be cool, Mike thought.

"Now I know that some of you have been asking for extra credit," Mrs. Canfield said, looking at Emily. "If you like, you may do your own experiment to show the class. I have a list of books and Web sites where you might find some ideas. Just remember: The experiment needs to show science from everyday life. You may only use materials that are already in your house or this classroom."

Extra credit? Mike was lucky if he finished the regular homework. He started to stare out the window again, when he remembered something. What had Nora said? "Bring home a really good report card."

That was too much to ask for. But an extra-credit project could make his report card look . . . better. Definitely! What if he got one really great grade this marking period? His parents would be so thrilled, they'd let him do whatever he wanted!

Plan B had just fallen into his lap, like magic.

Back at the beginning of the school year, Mike hated the idea of walking home with Nora. He didn't want people to see him going to her house. He didn't want people to see her coming to his house, either! In fourth grade, boys and girls weren't usually friends.

But now he knew there was something worse than walking home with Nora: walking home *without* Nora. He trudged through the neighborhood alone, kicking piles of leaves.

Nora had piano lessons today. And how was Mike supposed to come up with an extra-credit project on his own? Too bad he couldn't pull it out of thin air.

Mike's house was quiet. He poked his head into his mom's office. "Hey, Mike!" Mrs. Weiss said, taking off her glasses.

"Hey, Mom," he said. "Would it be okay if I borrowed your tablet?" That was the device his parents had made safe for him to browse. "I need to find some ideas for a science experiment."

"Sure," said his mom. "Let me know if you need a hand, okay?"

See? thought Mike. My own mom knows I can't do this on my own.

On the couch, Mike searched some of the sites that Mrs. Canfield had suggested. About a million ideas popped up on the computer screen. Mike could study light and vision by looking through a pickle jar full of water. He could make a small ball float in the warm air created by a hair dryer. Or he could make a geyser—a sort of liquid explosion—with soda and Mentos.

Candy science? That sounded good to Mike.

When he searched for candy and science together, he came up with another good idea. He could create electric sparks in his mouth by chewing some wintergreen Life Savers. Perfect!

Except that I'd have to keep my mouth open to show people the sparks, Mike thought. How many times would he have to do it? Maybe it would be too gross.

He came across a whole Web site full of experiments he could do with potatoes. A potato clock . . . a potato shooter . . . They were all great ideas, but Mike was looking for something that would make a big impression.

What about experiments that showed things about the human body? Taste tests . . . smell tests . . .

This was taking forever! Mike put his head down and yawned.

Yawning? Could that be an experiment? Or would it put people to sleep?

Mike went to his room to take a break.

He took a quarter off his dresser. To somebody else, it might look like spare change. To Mike, it was a training tool. Magicians had to practice their movements all the time to build the right muscles. It was just as important as homework. Or soccer practice. Mike had almost

PALMING a COIN

WITH YOUR RIGHT HAND, PALM AND FINGERS FACING UP, HOLD A COIN BETWEEN YOUR THUMB AND MIDDLE FINGER ALONG THE EDGE. THE REST OF YOUR FINGERS ARE HELD TIGHTLY TOGETHER. YOUR FINGERS SHOULD BE FACING THE AUDIENCE, WHILE YOUR THUMB IS FACING YOURSELF.

WITH YOUR LEFT HAND, REACH FOR THE COIN FROM ABOVE. YOUR LEFT HAND GRASPS THE COIN (OR AT LEAST IT APPEARS THAT WAY) WHILE, IN FACT, YOU LET THE COIN DROP INTO YOUR RIGHT PALM.

ONCE THE COIN IS IN YOUR RIGHT PALM, YOUR LEFT HAND SHOULD PRETEND TO GRASP THE COIN IN A FIST. AT THE SAME TIME, YOUR RIGHT HAND CLOSES JUST TIGHT ENOUGH TO HOLD THE HIDDEN COIN.

YOUR EYES MUST STAY FOCUSED ON YOUR LEFT FIST! YOU SHOULD SLOWLY MOVE IT TO THE LEFT SIDE OF YOUR BODY, WHILE YOUR BODY IS SLOWLY MOVING TO THE RIGHT, AND YOUR RIGHT ARM IS RELAXING ALONG THE RIGHT SIDE OF YOUR BODY.

SLOWLY RUB THE FINGERS OF YOUR LEFT FIST TOGETHER AS IF DISSOLVING THE COIN. OPEN YOUR LEFT HAND SLOWLY TO SHOW THE COIN HAS VANISHED!

5.

Note: *THE BEST WAY TO PRACTICE THIS MOVE IS TO ACTUALLY TAKE THE COIN WITH YOUR LEFT HAND USING ALL THE SAME MOVEMENTS. THEN SWITCH BACK AND FORTH BETWEEN TAKING THE COIN AND NOT TAKING IT. DOING THIS IN FRONT OF A MIRROR WILL HELP YOU UNDERSTAND HOW IT SHOULD REALLY LOOK WHEN YOU'RE ACTUALLY PALMING THE COIN.*

learned how to palm a coin—to make it disappear into the palm of his hand. Real magicians used this skill to hide coins when they needed to. It was everyday magic.

Which made Mike think of something.

You could do science with everyday stuff like baking soda and vinegar.

You could do magic with everyday stuff like water and ice cubes.

Could he do a magic trick to show some everyday science?

Maybe not with cards. Or coins. Or his new magic hat.

But Mike could show something unusual about the human body.

He didn't need Nora for this! He knew just what to do. He could demonstrate what it meant to be double-jointed! That was everyday science, no doubt about it. Double-jointed people were everywhere!

Of course . . . Mike wasn't one of them. But he could still show what it was all about. If only he knew how to do that thing that Carlos had showed him at the magic shop.

Too bad Mike couldn't just hop on his bike, go to The White Rabbit, and ask him.

Luckily, Mike just happened to have the world's most amazing book of magic tricks, right here in his room.

He dug *The Book of Secrets* out of its hiding place in his sock drawer. Mike wasn't even sure why he kept it hidden. It wasn't like his mom and dad would pick it up. It just didn't seem right to have a book like this on his bookshelf, where anyone could see. Magicians tried to protect the tricks of their trade.

Mr. Zerlin had given Mike *The Book of Secrets* right after they'd met. It was already old and worn, its pages soft from being turned so many times. Now there were sticky notes poking out

in every direction, marking pages Mike wanted to come back to. Almost everything Mike knew about magic came from this book. He went over the pictures and the directions again and again, until they were stuck in his mind with superglue.

There wasn't a table of contents. There wasn't an index. But the weirdest thing happened when Mike opened *The Book of Secrets* at random. The page he wanted was always right in front of him, like the book knew what he wanted. Today it fell open to the Incredible Twisting Arm.

Mike read the directions a couple of times. Then he put on a sweatshirt, like Carlos had worn at The White Rabbit, and stood in front of his bedroom mirror to try the trick for the first time.

It would probably take a while to get it right.

Chapter 6
PRACTICING

The next day, at recess, Mike met Zack and Charlie at their usual place on the playground. Most kids swarmed all over the climbing structure, but Mike and his friends played freezetag or kickball on the blacktop. Today, Charlie found a soccer ball under the slide.

Zack and Charlie had just finished up their soccer season, and they were still going over every detail of their final game.

"So . . . I was on defense, and I went . . ." Zack said, doing some fancy footwork with the ball.

"When Alex got that last goal, we knew we had it," Charlie added.

"Then the ball was in the air, and for some reason I just smacked it with my elbow," said Zack, showing Mike.

The thing was, Mike wasn't really into soccer anymore. Not since he'd discovered magic. He was glad his friends had won, but he didn't need to know the play-by-play. He looked around for something else to do.

Ten kids were standing in line to play four-square, but Mike didn't mind waiting. It would get him out of soccer for a while. And there was Nora, standing at the very end of the line. Mike couldn't wait to tell her he'd solved his problem without her. He wanted to bike alone to The White Rabbit, and now he knew just what to do to get his parents to let him.

As he headed for the line, though, Emily Winston glanced at the boys and walked over to Nora. She whispered something in Nora's ear, and the two girls started cracking up.

Fine, thought Mike. *I'm not playing with them! I hope Nora gets out on the first round.*

He was so busy scowling that he didn't notice the soccer ball flying through the air. Until it slammed into his face.

"I'm so sorry!" said Zack, rushing over. "It was an accident!"

"Do you need to get some ice?" Charlie asked urgently. "A Band-Aid?"

Mike felt his cheek to make sure he wasn't bleeding. It didn't seem like he was badly hurt. But his face was flushed with embarrassment.

"I'm okay," Mike assured his friends. "Seriously."

Nora rushed over from the four-square line. "I can take you to the nurse," she volunteered.

That was the last thing Mike wanted! "It's okay—I can go on my own," he said.

It was one thing to have people pay attention when he was doing

something cool, like making a cup float in midair. But Mike wasn't doing a show right now! He practically ran off the playground.

Inside Mrs. Rivard's office, another kid was throwing up into a trash can. Suddenly Mike felt like he had to throw up too. And that wasn't even the worst thing. After the kid washed up and came out of the bathroom, Mike saw who it was.

Jackson Jacobs, the biggest bully in the whole school.

Jackson Jacobs, who was big enough to be in junior high.

Jackson Jacobs, who totally had it in for Mike.

Mike pretended he didn't see Jackson. But when Jackson saw Mike, he smiled gleefully. Being mean to Mike was all the medicine he needed.

"Did baby get hurt on the playground?" Jackson said in some kind of creepy baby talk.

"A little boo-boo?" He came closer, like he was going to give Mike a hug. Knowing Jackson, though, it would be more like a headlock.

Mike backed away and used the only ammunition he had. "So *you* were the kid puking in the next room," Mike shot back.

Jackson didn't actually answer. He just got his big face up in Mike's and said, "Here's what I don't understand, Mike. You're so magical, right?" He sneered when he said the word. "And now you're in the nurse's office. If you have these . . . powers . . . why can't you just make yourself better?"

"That's not how it works," Mike said lamely.

Jackson's eyes narrowed. "That's because it doesn't work," he snapped. "It isn't magic. It's a *trick*. And I don't forget when people trick me, Weiss. You just wait." He turned to make sure no adults were around. "I'm gonna get you back sometime when you're not expecting it," he muttered. "Yeah . . . you'll see. . . ."

Mike had never been so happy to see the school nurse walk in with an ice pack. She held it up to his cheek and said, "You'll feel better in no time."

But what really made Mike feel better? The thing she said next, to Jackson. "Now, you come and rest until someone can take you home."

Nora came to Mike's house after school. He tried not to think about why she'd been laughing with Emily Winston.

As usual, they had snacks and spread their homework out on the kitchen table. Mike had to write a sentence with every one of his spelling words. It was going to take forever. Meanwhile, Nora did long division problems like a machine.

The minute she left, Mike rushed to his room to work on the Incredible Twisting Arm. He put on the sweatshirt and leaned down on his desk with all his weight. The first part of the trick felt weird, like he might hurt himself, but he figured out a way to do it that was pretty comfortable.

He twisted and twisted, watching his hand carefully. It went all the way around, like Carlos's had. Mike could even make that cracking sound, like crushed bones! Mrs. Canfield was going to love this.

After he demonstrated what it looked like to be double-jointed, he would share some scientific facts.

Being double-jointed didn't mean you had double joints, it turned out. It just meant that the joints you had—the places where two bones met—were extra flexible. Double-jointed people could bend their fingers backward and put their legs behind their heads. Turned out the condition was pretty common. It even ran in families.

Usually, Mike practiced magic in front of the mirror. But his desk was too far from the mirror to see. Maybe if he moved it a little closer . . .

Mrs. Weiss raced up the stairs when she heard the sound of Mike's desk grinding across the floor. "What's going on up here?" she asked. "Aren't you working on a science project?" she said.

"Yup," said Mike. "I just need to use the mirror. . . ."

His mom noticed *The Book of Secrets* lying open on the desk. "Looks like you're reading about magic," she said.

It was hard to explain. "It's science and magic all at once," Mike said.

Mrs. Weiss sat down on his bed.

“Remember what we talked about when school started?” she said. “About why soccer wasn’t a great idea this year?”

"Uh-huh," Mike said.

"Dad and I don't want anything to interfere with your schoolwork, Mike," said his mom. "We don't want you falling further behind. We want to see you building good habits."

Mrs. Weiss let out a deep breath. "I'm glad you've found a new hobby," she said, pointing to *The Book of Secrets.* "But it's just like it was with soccer. You can't let it get in the way of what's really important."

"But it is important!" Mike said. Magic meant a lot more to him than soccer ever did. "And I'm doing something magical . . . for school. Not just for school, Mom. For extra credit!"

It was like he'd said some magic words. "Extra credit?" she repeated.

"I'm working toward a goal, Mom," Mike explained. Her eyebrows went up with interest.

"If I get a good grade . . . a really good grade . . . I'm hoping to earn an extra privilege."

"You're too young for a cell phone, Mike," his mom said immediately, holding up her hand like a stop sign. "We've been over this before."

"Not a cell phone!" said Mike. "Actually . . . I was wondering if you and Dad might let me ride my bike downtown by myself. If I got a good grade on this project, you know. And showed how much I've been focusing on school." He didn't mention being mature or responsible, since that hadn't worked out so well.

His mom looked surprised. "What would you do downtown?" she asked.

Mike thought fast. "Go to . . . the library. And help with errands. And visit The White Rabbit, too," he added, as if that had just crossed his mind.

"All by yourself?" said his mom. "It's a long way. . . ."

Mike couldn't lose this chance. "I'd let you know when I was leaving," he said quickly. "I'd ride on the sidewalk, stop at every corner, never go too fast, never talk to strangers."

Mrs. Weiss stood up, like she was ready to leave. "Dad and I will think about it, Mike," she said. "I know he'll be happy to hear about this extra-credit project. And I know you'd like to be able to get to that magic shop. If we agreed to this—which is not definite," she cautioned, "we'd need to make some clear rules. Like homework first, magic second. Always."

"Got it," said Mike, playing it cool. He felt like he could dance around the room, though. All that stood between him and his freedom was one science project. One magic trick.

He knew he could do it.

BALANCE of POWER

WHILE NO ONE IS WATCHING, PUT A SMALL AMOUNT OF VASELINE OR LIP BALM ON THE TIP OF YOUR INDEX FINGER. THEN HAND A DECK OF CARDS TO YOUR AUDIENCE, BEING CAREFUL NOT TO TOUCH THE CARDS WITH YOUR STICKY FINGER. A SPECTATOR SHOULD CHOOSE TWO CARDS FROM THE DECK.

1.

TELL THE SPECTATOR THAT HE CAN KEEP ONE CARD AND GIVE THE OTHER TO YOU.

HOLD YOUR INDEX FINGER STRAIGHT UP IN THE AIR, KEEPING THE REST OF YOUR FINGERS CURLED TOWARD YOUR PALM. THE SPECTATOR SHOULD DO THE EXACT SAME THING.

KEEPING YOUR CARD HORIZONTAL AND LEVEL, PLACE IT ON TOP OF YOUR INDEX FINGER AND HOLD IT STEADY WITH YOUR OTHER HAND. AGAIN, THE SPECTATOR SHOULD DO THE SAME.

NOW, LET GO OF YOUR CARD AND WATCH IT REMAIN BALANCED ON YOUR INDEX FINGER. (THE VASELINE OR LIP BALM WILL HELP IT STAY IN PLACE.)

WHEN THE SPECTATOR GOES TO COPY YOU, THOUGH, HE WILL NOT BE ABLE TO DO THE SAME THING! HIS CARD MUST FOLLOW THE LAWS OF GRAVITY. YOURS, THOUGH, FOLLOWS THE LAWS OF MAGIC.

Chapter 7
WALKING ON AIR

The next morning, Mrs. Canfield stood in front of the class and smiled. "More than half of you have decided to do an extra-credit project," she said. "That's a lot of everyday science! Ms. Dorr and Mr. DeCamilla have had a lot of interest in their rooms, too. So now we have an exciting new idea."

Uh-oh, Mike thought. She can't cancel it, can she?

"Tomorrow, all three fourth-grade classes will meet to do an experiment together. Then, the students doing extra-credit projects will have a chance to share them with the whole grade! I'm sending home a flyer inviting your parents to join us if they like."

Mike's parents never came to school events during the day, since they were at work. But maybe they'd make an exception this time, Mike thought. This was a special occasion!

Emily Winston raised her hand. "What if we're not ready?" she asked.

Usually that was Mike's question. For the first time ever, though, he was prepared for an assignment ahead of time.

Mrs. Canfield reassured Emily and answered some other questions. Then she gathered the class around her desk in the front of the room. When everyone was quiet, she opened her drawer and took out a paper bag with something hidden inside.

"I know this is the last thing you'd ever expect to use in science," Mrs. Canfield said. "But this everyday object can show us an interesting scientific property."

The thing in the bag? It was a diaper!

"Diapers contain a substance that acts like a giant sponge," said Mrs. Canfield. "Today we're going to see just how much liquid a diaper can absorb—and why!"

For once, Mike wasn't spacing out or goofing off. He really wanted to know what they would do with a diaper. He was actually paying attention!

Mrs. Canfield handed around diapers from several different brands. Some were for tiny babies, some were for bigger kids to wear overnight.

She also passed out bottles of water, with droppers. "We're going to put water onto the diapers drop by drop, until they can't hold any more," she explained. "At first it will seem like nothing is happening, but pretty soon your diaper will get big and bulky."

"Just like a real one!" someone called out. For once, it wasn't Mike.

Mike did what he was told, and quietly. Drop by drop, he filled the diaper . . . until it broke open at the sides and started oozing some kind of gooey beads.

"Mrs. Canfield!" he yelled. "I have a problem here!"

She rushed over to help. Then she smiled. "Mike has uncovered the material that makes diapers possible," she said. "A special kind of plastic."

Okay, Mike didn't really want to be the kid with the exploding diaper. But nothing could bother Mike today. Not being covered in oozing plastic. Not even Jackson Jacobs scowling at him from the classroom next door when he went to the boys' room to wash his hands.

Jackson could scowl all he wanted, Mike thought. He didn't care. He was getting extra credit!

All day, he went through school with what his grandma would call an extra spring in his step. What did that mean, anyway? Bouncing with happiness, Mike figured. Walking on air.

He put Mrs. Canfield's flyer in his coat pocket, so he wouldn't forget to give it to his mom and dad. Most days, Mike couldn't wait for the bell to ring at three o'clock. Today, though? He couldn't wait to go back tomorrow!

Nora's family had the world's worst snacks. Plain popcorn, anyone? No salt, no butter, no nothing. Sitting at her kitchen table, Mike devoured a whole bowl of it. No, not even this popcorn could get him down.

Nora was making her way through a worksheet. But

Mike couldn't do his homework. For one thing, he was too excited. And wouldn't he get a break on the regular homework, since he was doing the extra-credit project? That seems only fair, Mike thought.

"Hey, Nora," he said. "Remember that magic trick I was trying to teach you? We need to practice!"

Nora put down her pencil. "Oh, yeah!" she said. "The one where I'm your partner?"

Mike grinned. With Nora as his partner, he knew the trick would work.

"All right," said Mike, getting back to where they'd left off. "Remember . . . I've asked some-one to pick a card. Now I'm calling my mysterious friend on the phone. Her name is Ms. Magus, and she can tell what the card is without even seeing it! So you're the friend, of course. I'll call you, somehow. And then I'll tell you what the card is, without the audience knowing what I'm doing. It's like a secret code."

"Okay," said Nora. "So what's the code?"

Mike explained. "I'll say 'Hello, may I speak to Ms. Magus?' On your end of the phone, you'll start counting slowly. Say all the numbers in a deck of cards, from ace to king. When I interrupt you, you'll know you've just said the right one."

Nora nodded. She got it right away.

"And we do the same thing for the suits," Mike added. "Clubs, diamonds, spades, hearts. You say them one by one, and when I cut you off, you'll know you've got it."

"Great!" said Nora.

"So . . . say the card is six of hearts," Mike said.

Nora started counting. "Ace . . . two . . . three . . . four . . . five . . ."

When she got to six, Mike said, "Hello, Ms. Magus!" like she had just picked up the phone.

Nora didn't miss a beat. She started right in on the suits until, again, Mike cut her off. "I'll say something when you get there. And then I'll give the phone to the person who picked the card."

"Perfect!" Nora said. "Except for one thing. We still have to figure out the phone. Like . . . how can we do this at school?"

"I know," Mike said. It was definitely a problem. The way his day was going, though, he had a good feeling it would all work out. "We'll just see what happens," he said. "Wait till we know there's a phone, I guess."

"That's all we can do," said Nora, returning to her worksheet.

But Mike didn't want to get back to work. All he could think about was magic, and how it was about to save the day for him! With a magic trick, he'd earn extra credit. With extra credit, he'd earn a new privilege. Magic would get him to the magic shop!

"So do you want to see my extra-credit science experiment?" Mike said. "I've been working really hard on it."

"Sure!" said Nora. "What's it about?"

"Double-jointedness," Mike said. "You know, it's what lets some people bend their fingers back, or put their legs up behind their heads." He'd have to think of a better way to say that before tomorrow.

"A girl at my old school was double-jointed," Nora said. "She could move her thumb in a perfect circle." Obviously, she knew what he was talking about.

"So watch this," Mike said. He'd taken off his sweatshirt when he walked into Nora's house, but now he put it back on. Just like he'd practiced, he put his right hand down on the table, fingers facing toward the left. Putting all his weight on the hand, he began to twist it toward his body.

MIND MELD

For this trick, you need a partner you can trust. Your partner will agree to play the part of your mysterious friend, Ms. Magus, on the other end of a phone.

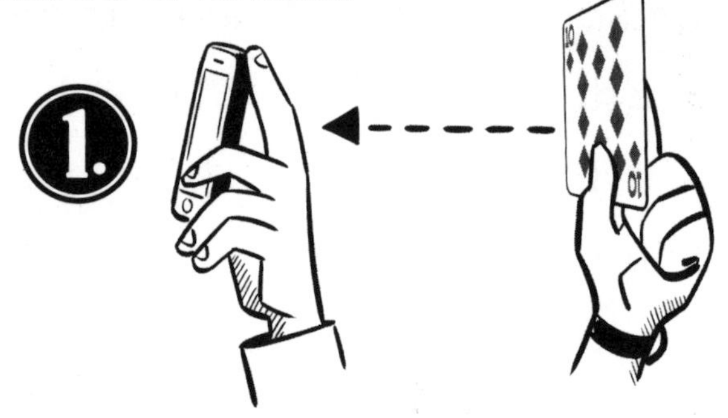

Ask a member of your audience to pick a card from a deck and show it to you. Your friend, Ms. Magus, will know what the card is, even though she is many miles away. (Tell the audience that *magus* is another word for 'sorcerer.')

Call your friend on the phone. When she picks up, you say, "Hello, may I please speak to Ms. Magus?"

YOU PRETEND YOU'RE WAITING FOR HER TO COME TO THE PHONE, BUT REALLY SHE'S ALREADY THERE, COUNTING SLOWLY LIKE THIS: ACE, 2, 3, 4, 5, 6, 7, 8, 9, 10, JACK, QUEEN, KING. WHEN SHE GETS TO THE NUMBER THAT'S ON THE CARD, YOU INTERRUPT BY SAYING, "HELLO, MS. MAGUS!" LIKE SHE HAS JUST PICKED UP.

WHEN SHE HEARS THAT LINE, SHE WILL SAY THE NAMES OF THE FOUR SUITS IN A DECK OF CARDS: HEARTS, DIAMONDS, SPADES, CLUBS. WHEN SHE GETS TO THE ONE THAT MATCHES THE CARD IN YOUR HAND, YOU'LL SAY, "HOLD ON, PLEASE." THAT IS HER CLUE THAT SHE HAS THE RIGHT SUIT.

NOW, SHE KNOWS EXACTLY WHAT THE CARD IS, AND SHE CAN TALK TO THE AUDIENCE MEMBER WHO CHOSE THE CARD. HAND THE PHONE TO THE SPECTATOR. MS. MAGUS WILL NAME THE CARD IN HER BEST SORCERER VOICE—AND THE SPECTATOR WILL BE AMAZED BY THE POWER OF HER MIND MAGIC.

Nora's reaction was kind of like Mike's when he saw Carlos do this at The White Rabbit. At first she looked at him like, "What's the big deal?" As he twisted his hand all the way around, though, her eyes widened until they were bulging out of her head. She jumped when she heard the cracking noise.

"Yikes!" she said. "Are you okay?"

"It's killing me," Mike said, shaking his hand out like Carlos had. "But yeah, I'm okay. After I show everyone, I'll tell them some facts about being double-jointed. It doesn't mean what people think, you know. Nobody has two joints. It's just that double-jointed people can move their bodies in ways that most people can't."

Nora was listening intently, so Mike threw in one more fact. "A fancy name for the condition is hypermobility," he said. He even said the word without messing up.

Nora shook her head. "That's crazy," she said. "I can't believe you can do that. I had no idea you were double-jointed!"

"Oh," Mike said. "I'm not really double-jointed! I'm just . . . showing what it means to be."

For a couple of seconds, Nora was quiet. Then she said, "So you're pretending."

"I'm demonstrating what it's all about," Mike said.

"So it's not really an experiment," said Nora. "It's more like a magic trick."

"Well . . . yes," Mike replied. "But lots of people are double-jointed. So it's everyday science, too." Didn't she see?

But what Nora saw was something that hadn't even crossed Mike's mind. "I don't think you can do that for extra credit," she said slowly. "Isn't it sort of . . . lying?"

Chapter 8
PLAYGROUND MAGIC

So what in the world was he supposed to do now? It wasn't like Mike had some notebook full of science experiments just hanging around. This magic trick . . . it was his only good idea. Ever. And now he wasn't sure if he could use it.

Mike didn't really think it was lying. So what if he wasn't double-jointed himself? Lots of other people were. The fact that he was doing a *trick* . . . that didn't really matter.

But what if Mrs. Canfield thought it was lying? Then he'd be right back in the principal's office. With no extra credit.

And what if his parents thought it was lying? He'd be in major trouble. He'd never get to go to The White Rabbit on his own. He might not get to go there *at all.*

"Lights out," said his dad, walking into Mike's bedroom. "Tomorrow's a big day!" Mike's parents had practically ripped Mrs. Canfield's flyer out of his hand when he came home. "Of course we'll be there!" they said. "We wouldn't miss it!" They acted like it was no big deal to reorganize their schedules.

So now his room was dark, but Mike couldn't get to sleep. He tossed and turned and worried. He didn't know how to handle this. He needed some advice. He already knew what Nora thought. He didn't want to worry his mom and dad. So who else was there?

Zack? Charlie? They'd be in bed by now. Mr. Zerlin? Mike had no clue how to reach him. And how would he explain that to his parents? To them, Mr. Zerlin was a total stranger. Not someone to chat with when it was—Mike checked his clock—after ten at night.

Mike heard his parents turn off the TV and come upstairs to sleep, but he was as wide awake as ever. After a while, he sat up and felt under his bed for a flashlight. Its thin beam lit the room just enough for Mike to find *The Book of Secrets* and take it out of his sock drawer.

Doing a different magic trick wasn't going to help him, Mike knew. So what was he looking for? He wasn't exactly sure. But *The Book of Secrets* always showed him what he wanted. And it was no different tonight. The book fell open to a page at the very beginning, part of the introduction.

"There is more to magic than smooth moves or perfect timing," Mike read. "The real magic is in the performance. A good magician is an actor. A storyteller. An entertainer! The magician's confidence is key to a successful show."

Mike sighed. It was too late to come up with a new project. He'd just have to pretend he was confident and believe in the one he had.

The whole fourth grade was squeezed into Mr. DeCamilla's room, working on their last experiment. Mike and another kid, Ben, had a small plastic bag full of milk, cream, and sugar sealed inside a larger bag full of ice and rock salt. "This is supposed to make ice cream?" Mike said doubtfully.

Ben looked at their instruction sheet. "Okay. We need to take the temperature of the ice, then shake the bags gently for about ten minutes." He stuck a thermometer into the ice and wrote the number down.

Mike grabbed the bags. "Ten minutes?" he said. "Maybe it won't take so long if we shake them harder. . . ."

When he gave the bags a real shake, milk squirted all over the place, like ketchup that was stuck in a bottle. Ben stared at him.

"How about I do that?" Ben suggested. "And then you can take the temperature when it's all done."

"Okay," said Mike. He stood there for a while, watching while Ben shook the bags his own way. At this rate, they wouldn't have ice cream until tomorrow.

Mike paced to the front of the room. After all the fourth graders made ice cream, they'd have their afternoon recess. Then their parents would arrive and the extra-credit projects would begin. When the projects were done, they'd all eat the ice cream together.

There was a list on Mr. DeCamilla's wall, showing the order the kids would go in. Mike was near the middle, right after Zack and Charlie. Hey, thought Mike. I didn't know we could team up! He would have teamed up with Nora, of course. That was a no-brainer! She'd probably get *extra* extra credit. Where was she on the list, anyway? And what was her project? Suddenly, he realized he didn't know.

Mike scanned the list until he found her name. Right near the top, and not alone. Nora had a partner, all right. But it wasn't Mike. It was Emily Winston.

He didn't get a chance to talk to Nora until they were filing out for recess. Mike pushed his way into the line right in front of her.

"You're doing your project with Emily Winston?" he asked, turning around. Nora looked at the floor. "Why didn't you tell me?"

"I can tell you don't like her," Nora said. "And you and I don't have to be partners all the time."

"I know!" Mike replied quickly. "It's just that she's such a know-it-all. . . ."

But a know-it-all partner could be a good thing, Mike realized.

Better than a partner who knew nothing. Like him.

"Well, I think she's nice," said Nora firmly. "We have fun jumping rope. And she reminds me of my best friend from my old school, okay?"

Mike acted like it didn't bother him. "Fine," he said. "Just . . . well . . . it didn't have to be a secret."

"I'm sorry, Mike," said Nora.

Can we ever be partners again? Mike wondered. He depended on Nora more than he wanted to admit.

He had an answer almost right away. "Listen . . ." said Nora. She lowered her voice so nobody else in the line could hear her. "Emily has a cell phone, and she says we can use it. No questions asked. What if I'm Ms. Magus at recess?"

♠ ♠ ♠

Having one phone, actually, wasn't quite enough. If Mike was on the playground with Emily's phone, where would Nora be?

He should have known she would figure that out.

"I asked Mrs. Rivard if I could make a call," Nora said. Everyone knew the school nurse would let you call from her office if you left something home. The school secretary would give you a hard time about it, but Mrs. Rivard wouldn't bother you. She really wanted you to have your sneakers for gym, or your instrument for band, or whatever. If you thought you could reach your parents, she'd let you call.

"Isn't that lying?" Mike replied pointedly.

"It's one minute on the phone," Nora said. "Do you want to do it or not?"

Of course Mike wanted to do it. Even with Emily Winston's help. He couldn't quite meet Emily's eyes as she handed him her cell phone at the door.

"Thanks," Mike mumbled. He made his way to the blacktop and waited for Zack and Charlie.

When the boys came out, Zack was dribbling a basketball. He passed it to Charlie, who looked at Mike. But Mike put his hands up to show he was busy with something else. He was holding a deck of cards.

"Hey, guys, can I show you something?" he said.

Zack and Charlie ran over. They knew they were about to be amazed.

"Just pick a card, any card," Mike said, holding out the deck to Zack.

Zack picked the one that was second from the top. "Can I tell you what it is?" he asked.

Mike nodded. "Okay," said Zack. "It's the ten of diamonds."

"Now, listen to this," said Mike. "I have a friend named Ms. Magus, a mind-reader so magnificent that she can tell what you're thinking without even seeing you. She can detect your brain waves over the phone!"

Even if they suspected it was Nora, they wouldn't know how it all worked.

"So I'm going to call Ms. Magus at home, see if she can work her magic for us," Mike continued. Doing a little show like this . . . it made him forget about the extra-credit project for now. He felt confident and in control, just like *The Book of Secrets* said.

A couple of other kids came over to see what they were doing. Emily, of course. And Ben. And Jackson Jacobs, who stood there with his arms crossed.

Mike dialed a number on Emily's phone, taking care that nobody could see the numbers or guess that he was really calling Mrs. Rivard's office.

Nora picked up after two rings, and Mike said, "Hello! May I please speak to Ms. Magus?" just as they'd planned.

He pretended he was waiting patiently for Ms. Magus to come to the phone. Meanwhile, on the other end, Nora was counting softly. When she finally got to ten, Mike broke into a smile and said, "Hello, Ms. Magus!" That was Nora's clue to stop. Now she knew the card was a ten.

Mike pretended to have a little conversation with her. "We're at recess, and I'm here with a bunch of other kids," he said. "My friend Zack just picked a card from my deck, and I'm calling to see if you can tell me what it is."

10♦

At the same time, Nora whispered the suits into the phone. "Hearts . . . spades . . . clubs . . . diamonds."

When she got to diamonds, Mike said, "Hold on a second, okay?" and again that was the clue. Diamonds.

Mike handed the phone to Zack. "Ms. Magus is ready to talk to you," he explained. "Can I put it on speaker?" Zack nodded, and Mike pushed a button on Emily's phone. The kids all gathered around to hear it.

Nora put on a creaky voice, like a voice on an old radio. "I can feel it," she said as Ms. Magus. "It's coming to me now. Is it a . . . ten of diamonds?"

Zack looked at Mike. "It is!"

"Thank you, Ms. Magus," Mike said. "Your powers are as strong as ever." He ended the call and handed the phone back to Emily, beaming.

"But how did you do that?" Zack asked, shaking his head.

Mike never knew what to say when people asked that. Did they really think he was going to tell?

He didn't even get a chance to answer, because Jackson butted in. "He tricked you, that's how," he snarled. "You can't trust Mike Weiss. You know that, don't you?"

And then the bell rang. Recess was over. It was time for another kind of show.

Chapter 9

THE INCREDIBLE TWISTING ARM

Mrs. Canfield stood in front of the whole fourth grade. Now they were in the cafeteria, since all the lunch periods were over. "Welcome, fourth graders," she said. "And welcome, parents!"

Mike's mom and dad were at a table in the corner. When Mike glanced over at them, his mom winked encouragingly.

"When we started our unit on everyday science," said Mrs. Canfield, "the teachers had no idea the students would be so enthusiastic! We've spent the week doing experiments in our classrooms and writing reports about them. Then, earlier today, the three classes came together to complete one special project."

No one was supposed to tell the parents about the ice cream.

"We never expected that so many children would try to earn extra credit," Mrs. Canfield continued. "Perhaps they all feel they need to earn higher grades," she said. "But I like to think it's mostly that they're excited about everyday science!"

Or a little bit of both, Mike thought.

Mrs. Canfield was wrapping up her introduction. "Before we begin, I just want to explain that this is not a science fair, with many weeks to get ready. The goal is just for us to see the ways that we encounter science every day. Each student will show us some science from ordinary life, and tell us a little bit about it. All of these projects use materials that are easy to find at home."

She looked at the list that Mike had seen on the wall. "We'll start with . . . Nora Finn and Emily Winston."

Mike had to admit their project was pretty cool. Emily took out a box of cereal and poured some into a bowl. Then Nora took out a giant magnet and showed that you could use it to attract the cereal flakes.

Why was that? There was a mineral called iron in the flakes. It was almost the same as the iron you'd find in, say, nails—but it was also something that people needed to eat. Lots of cereal boxes said "Fortified with iron" on them, and this was what it meant. "Everyday science starts with breakfast," Nora finished, and everyone applauded.

She would have been an excellent science partner, Mike thought. But maybe it was enough to have her as a magic partner instead.

The only bad thing about watching them was that it made him worry about his own demonstration all over again. He took off his sweatshirt, even though it was an important part of the Incredible Twisting Arm. Mike was so nervous that he was getting sweaty.

Zack and Charlie were up pretty soon after the girls. They mixed a weird goop out of corn-starch and water. It was hard to see what was special about it, so they passed it around the cafeteria. It looked like glue, Mike thought. But when he poked it, the goop didn't move. It was solid, like a piece of plastic.

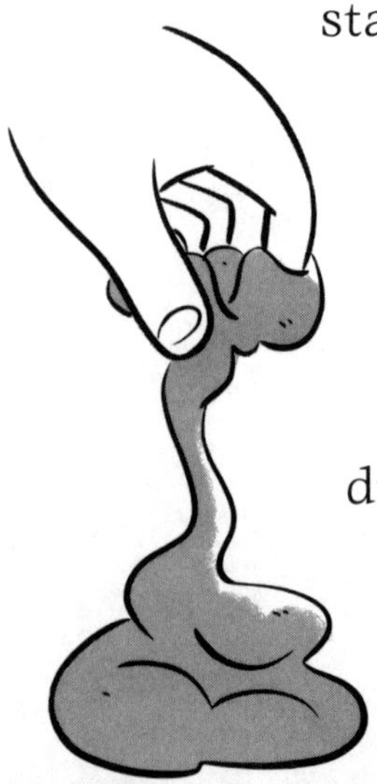

Zack and Charlie said that some liquids would change texture if you heated them up or cooled them down. This one, though, changed to a solid when you touched it. You could even slap it and it wouldn't splatter!

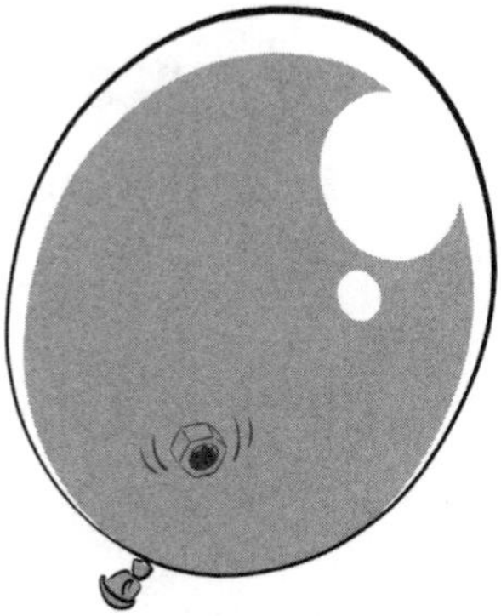

Even Jackson Jacobs wanted extra credit. His experiment was not so popular with the teachers, though. He blew up a balloon with a hex nut inside it—a little piece of hardware from his dad's tool bench. Then he spun the balloon around in the air, and the hex nut inside made a terrible noise, like screaming. He was trying to show something about sound. But Mr. DeCamilla cut him off quickly. "Thank you, Jackson," he said.

Finally, it was Mike's turn. He quickly put his sweatshirt back on and walked to the front of the cafeteria. "I don't . . . um . . . have any special equipment," he said. "I'm just going to demonstrate something unusual about the human body. Some people . . . um . . . can't even touch their toes. . . ."

He met his mom's gaze. Where in the world are you going with this? her eyes asked.

Mike took a deep breath. "But other people are extra-flexible," he went on. "We call those people double-jointed. Like this!"

Now that the talking was out of the way, Mike felt better. And what did *The Book of Secrets* say? Confidence is the key to success, or something? Mike definitely felt confident about the magic trick. He'd practiced it so many times now, he could do it just as well as Carlos.

So he did the trick just the same way he'd done it in front of the mirror. The same way he'd done it for Nora, too. He began with all his weight on the arm, and twisted it toward his body. As usual, it didn't look like much at first.

The INCREDIBLE TWISTING ARM

START BY WEARING A LONG-SLEEVE BAGGY SHIRT OR A LONG-SLEEVE JACKET.

1. WHILE YOUR RIGHT ARM IS SLACK ALONGSIDE YOUR BODY, TWIST YOUR RIGHT WRIST CLOCKWISE AS FAR AS POSSIBLE. YOU MUST DO THIS WITHOUT ANYONE NOTICING!

2. IN THAT TWISTED POSITION, PLACE YOUR HAND PALM-DOWN ON A SURFACE IN FRONT OF YOURSELF, LIKE THE FLOOR (IN WHICH CASE, YOU'LL NEED TO KNEEL DOWN) OR A TABLE. IT MAY BE EASIER TO USE YOUR LEFT HAND TO GRASP YOUR RIGHT WRIST TO HELP PLACE IT ON THE SURFACE. LEAN YOUR WEIGHT SLIGHTLY ON THE RIGHT HAND. YOUR FINGERS SHOULD BE POINTING TO THE LEFT.

   THE LONG SLEEVE WILL HIDE THE FACT THAT YOUR ARM IS ALREADY TWISTED.

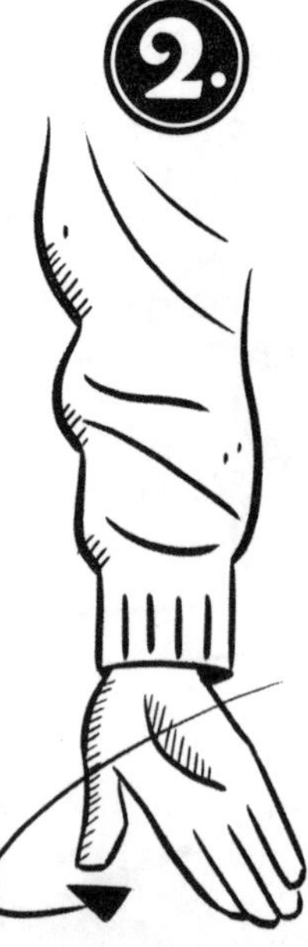

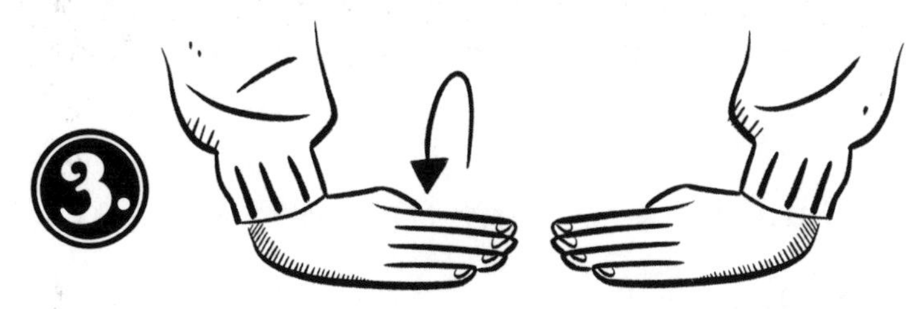

NOW, PLACE YOUR LEFT HAND IN FRONT OF YOURSELF AS WELL, WITH FINGERS POINTING TO THE RIGHT. YOUR HANDS SHOULD BE FACING EACH OTHER.

TELL YOUR SPECTATORS TO WATCH YOUR RIGHT HAND. SLOWLY BEGIN TO TURN YOUR RIGHT HAND COUNTERCLOCKWISE, WHICH SHOULD BE TOWARD YOURSELF. KEEP TURNING AND TURNING VERY SLOWLY. ACT AS IF IT IS SLIGHTLY PAINFUL. CONTINUE TURNING THE HAND UNTIL IT TURNS NO FURTHER.

NOW, IT LOOKS LIKE YOU'VE COMPLETELY TWISTED IT AROUND!

IF YOU WISH TO CREATE A CRACKING SOUND, PLACE A HARD PLASTIC CUP UNDER YOUR LEFT ARMPIT. SQUEEZE DOWN ON THE CUP, CRACKING IT, WHENEVER YOU FEEL IT'S APPROPRIATE.

But as he spun it past the halfway point, one of the mothers covered her mouth in surprise.

"Would you grab my fingers?" Mike asked Mrs. Canfield. It was an extra idea he had, all of a sudden, to make the trick more dramatic. "Could you push them that way?" He pointed with his head.

"I don't want to hurt you. . . ." his teacher said.

"It's okay," said Mike. "I do it all the time."

As she pushed, he made the bone-cracking sound, and somebody gasped. Then, at last, the fingers were right back where they'd started. The cafeteria was quiet. Success!

"I've never seen anything quite like that," said Mrs. Canfield, stunned. "So, can you tell us exactly what it means to be double-jointed?"

Mike repeated that fact about how nobody actually has double joints, but some joints are looser than others. "And it's a pretty common thing," Mike added. "If your parents are double-jointed, there's a good chance you will be too."

He didn't look at his own parents. He still wasn't sure what they'd think of this project. Any minute, though, it would all be over. Mike Weiss would no longer need improvement. He'd have extra credit!

Then someone in the cafeteria put a hand up. "I have a question," said a boy Mike didn't know. "When did you figure out you were double-jointed?"

For a second, Mike thought he would lie. But how could he, when his mom and dad were sitting right there? They knew he wasn't double-jointed. Maybe it was lying, like Nora said, to do a magic trick for a science project in the first place. He couldn't tell another lie too.

So Mike stammered, "Well . . . I'm not actually double-jointed. I was just trying to . . . show everyone what that would be like. . . ."

Now the boy was totally confused. "If you're not double-jointed, how did you . . ."

Jackson's voice drowned out the rest of his question. "Oh, I know what he did!" he yelled triumphantly. "That wasn't a science project! *That was a magic trick!*"

All of Mike's confidence drained away when Jackson opened his big mouth. Now he was just a kid trying to get away with something.

Mike met his mother's eyes again. He had some explaining to do.

And Mrs. Canfield? She looked disappointed. Like she had expected more from Mike.

Then another voice piped up.

Sometimes it was good to have a know-it-all in the audience.

"Isn't there a lot of science in magic?" said Emily Winston. "I saw a cool exhibit about that at the science museum."

Of all people, Mike couldn't believe that Emily was the one to save him.

And another lucky thing? He had practically memorized what *The Book of Secrets* said about science.

"Actually, yes!" said Mike. "Magic seems to defy the laws of science, right? Things that can't happen, happen. Things disappear, or float in the air. Suddenly, something happens, and you can't believe your eyes."

He looked to make sure his parents were listening.

"But magicians actually use science in their tricks. They confuse our senses on purpose. They make it seem like they've changed the way the world works. But they really just change the way we see it."

He knew what everyone wanted to know, but he still couldn't tell them.

"So the trick I just showed you . . . I can't say how it works. Magicians always keep their secrets secret," Mike explained. "I can tell you this, though: It's an optical illusion. What you see is not exactly what it seems."

And that was the end of it. "I'd like to learn more about this, Mike," Mrs. Canfield said. "Thank you for sharing your magic with the fourth grade. Jada, I think you're up next."

♠ ♠ ♠

Mike and his parents ate their ice cream silently. He knew they'd be having a big talk when he got home that afternoon. And what could he say? Next time, he'd listen to Nora.

Mrs. Canfield came over with some chocolate sauce. "Would you like some?" she said to Mrs. Weiss.

"No thanks," said Mike's mom. "And our apologies about Mike's project," she added. "Of course we had no idea it was a magic trick."

"Actually, I'd like to see more of Mike's optical illusions this year," said Mrs. Canfield brightly. "This is very interesting stuff!"

"We just don't want magic to interfere with Mike's schoolwork," Mr. Weiss said, like Mike wasn't sitting right there.

"Oh, no. Quite the opposite!" Mrs. Canfield replied. "I think that magic could be *helping* with his schoolwork. Without magic, I'm not sure Mike would have pushed himself to try for extra credit. I am so pleased with his progress. He earned ten extra points today!"

She turned to Mike, ruffled his hair, and said, "Nice job!"

Chapter 10

ON HIS OWN

On Saturday morning, Mike wheeled his bike out of the driveway and adjusted his helmet. *Okay, this is pretty weird,* he thought. *I can't believe I'm actually doing this!*

"So you know how to get there, right?" said his dad from the porch.

"And you'll let us know as soon as you arrive?" his mom added. She'd called The White Rabbit

ahead of time to make sure that Mike could use the store phone.

"Yes and yes," said Mike. He was already thinking about the next time there was an extra-credit project. If he did well—without a magic trick!—maybe he'd finally get a phone of his own.

"Don't stay too long," said his mom.

"Be sure to let us know when you're on your way back," said his dad.

Enough already! thought Mike. He waved to them and pedaled down the street. There was a cool breeze in his face and a light feeling in his heart. *This* is the new me, Mike thought. Not so mature. Not so responsible. But good enough to handle this.

He biked by Nora's house and Charlie's house. He put on a burst of speed when he went by Jackson's.

Mike coasted to a stop at the corner with the blinking light. He looked both ways and crossed. Then he saw a girl ahead of him, walking a dog. It was Emily Winston, with Pookie. She'd been absent on the day after the science presentations. Mike hadn't seen or talked to her since.

Mike pedaled slowly until he caught up. "Hey, Emily," he said. "You totally saved me the other day. Thanks for remembering that exhibit about the Science of Magic!"

Pookie wagged her tail when Mike patted her. "It's okay," Emily said. "I'm glad you didn't get in trouble."

"Yeah, me too," said Mike. He stood there, hanging out with Emily's dog for a minute. What else was he supposed to say? He had someplace important to be!

"So, um, have a great day," Mike said. As he headed off again, he waved. We don't really

have to be friends, he thought. Just . . . friendly. That's enough for now.

When he finally arrived at The White Rabbit, Mike chained his bike to the rack outside the store and walked right in. For the first time ever, he'd be at the shop without his parents moving him along.

Carlos was at the counter. "Hey, Mike!" he said. Carlos knew what to do next. "Here's the phone!"

Mike dialed his home number. "I'm alive and well," he said when his mom answered. "Yes! I'll call you when I'm leaving."

When he hung up, he turned to Carlos. "So I learned that arm-twisting trick," he bragged.

"It's a good one, right?" said Carlos.

"Great effect," Mike said, nodding. Carlos didn't need to know the rest of the story.

Mike drifted off into the back room, to browse for as long as he wanted. He couldn't believe he hadn't seen that glass case on the wall before, full of old-time handcuffs. Did someone use them for an escape? Mike wondered. Usually kids didn't do escape acts. But maybe someday . . .

And here was a bin full of dice, all different kinds. Some were just normal, like you'd use to play Monopoly. Some were trick dice, that would add up to the same number no matter how you rolled them. And some of them were crazy shapes, with way more than six sides. All together, they looked like a bowl of gems, their many sides glinting in the light.

Mike must have spent an hour in there, looking at drawers full of magic tricks, neatly labeled. Every time he'd been at

The White Rabbit before, his parents or Nora had rushed him right past these. But not today! Mike didn't even know what all this stuff did, but he had a feeling he'd find out. Appearing canes. Mouth coils. A silk fountain. Flash paper. It was all a new language Mike was dying to speak.

A bell jingled above the door to announce that someone else was walking in. Mike looked up. He couldn't believe it! It was that kid from the science presentations, the one he didn't know. The one who asked the question that almost ruined everything!

The kid looked thrilled to see him. "I can't believe you're here!" he said to Mike. "I loved that arm twist you did at school, and I started thinking I wanted to learn some magic, too. Oh, I'm in Ms. Dorr's class. My name is Adam."

Mike was showing Adam a simple card trick when Mr. Zerlin walked in.

"Greetings," he said to Adam, like he knew he was new here. He was wearing a hat today. A fedora, Mike thought it was called. One of those hats that old men and cool teenagers wore. Mike didn't think much of it until Mr. Zerlin took it off and reached inside. He handed Adam a bunch of fresh flowers. "You're always welcome at The White Rabbit," he said.

Adam looked at Mike. "Whoa!" he said. "How did he do that?"

Mike wasn't telling. Not yet.

At some point Carlos came into the back room. "Mike," he said, "your mom is getting worried. . . ."

Mike didn't want to leave. But if his mom was worried, she wouldn't let him come again. "I better go," he said to Adam. "See you at school on Monday!" He wondered what Adam liked to do at recess. Mike was really getting sick of soccer.

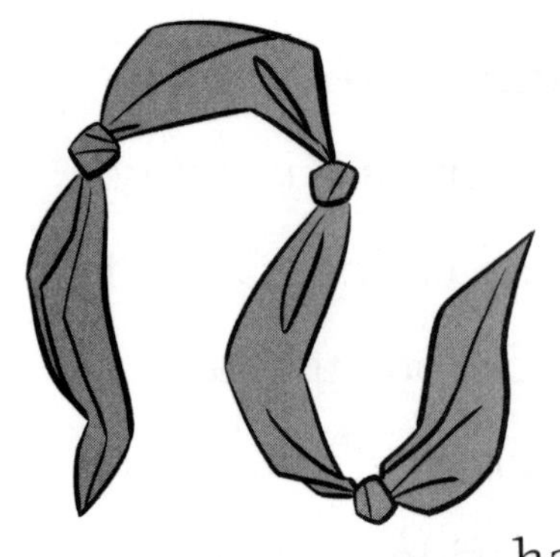

Mike was only buying a few magic silks today, since he could stuff those in his pockets for the bike ride home. Silks were like handkerchiefs, only slippery. Magicians used them for tons of things.

"Glad you could come," said Mr. Zerlin. He didn't finish the sentence with "on your own," but Mike was pretty sure that's what he meant.

While Mr. Zerlin rang him up, Mike noticed a photo hanging on the wall behind him. It was of a short, muscular man, glaring intensely at the camera. Mike got the feeling the guy in the picture was really looking at *him.* His eyes were light and bright, and his stare . . . well, it looked like he couldn't be distracted by a herd of elephants.

"Who's that?" Mike asked, pointing.

Mr. Zerlin gave him a handful of change. "Erik Weisz," he said.

Who? Mike wondered.

"Harry Houdini," continued Mr. Zerlin. "Who had the same last name as yours, before he changed it."

Oh yeah, Mike thought. He'd done a report on Houdini, but he'd never seen him looking so . . . mysterious. That was pretty amazing, actually. He had the same last name as the greatest magician of all time? What were the chances of that?

He smiled at Mr. Zerlin. "Thanks," he said. "I'll be back soon. Like . . . maybe tomorrow."

Mr. Zerlin tipped his hat, like someone in an old movie, as Mike walked toward the door.

Back at his house, his mom was on the phone with his grandma. His dad was grading papers. It was a regular Saturday for them, even though it was a special day for Mike.

He opened the cupboard, found a box of cookies, and sneaked them up to his room. His parents liked people to eat in the kitchen, but the cookies would be gone before his mom and dad knew what happened.

Mike settled into his beanbag chair and opened *The Book of Secrets*. What could he do with the silks? Well, he could scrunch them up and make them appear from the end of his wand. He could tie them together and magically make them untie. He could make them change color, change places, and multiply. All with a lot of practice.

And what about that hat trick Mr. Zerlin did? Mike wondered. He had his own hat now. He should find a way to use it, right? Mike didn't have any flowers around, but he could work with anything that would fit inside the hat.

Mike took the hat off the floor of his closet, where he'd left it. He turned it upside down and looked inside. How big was the secret compartment, anyway? he wondered. How much room did he have to work with?

He noticed a couple of things when he gave the hat a closer look.

For one thing, there was more than one compartment. He could hide a few things in there at once. Maybe some of the silks?

The other thing was that there was a tag inside one of the other compartments. It had some letters on it. Initials? His grandma said this hat came from some cousin of hers, right? Who used it when he was young, learning magic. Someone with the initials E. W.

Mike's first thought was Emily Winston. There was an E. W. who would never own a magic hat!

But then he remembered that picture at The White Rabbit, and Mike got goose bumps. Believe? Well, this was unbelievable!

E. W. was also Erik Weisz.

E.W.

Thank you for reading this FEIWEL AND FRIENDS book.
The Friends who made

possible are:

Jean Feiwel, *Publisher*
Liz Szabla, *Editor in Chief*
Rich Deas, *Senior Creative Director*
Holly West, *Associate Editor*
Dave Barrett, *Executive Managing Editor*
Nicole Liebowitz Moulaison, *Production Manager*
Lauren A. Burniac, *Editor*
Anna Roberto, *Associate Editor*

FOLLOW US ON FACEBOOK OR VISIT US ONLINE AT MACKIDS.COM.